This book belongs to

. . . .

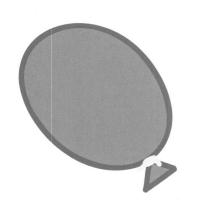

Peppa Pig

Published by Ladybird Books Ltd 2013
A Penguin Company
Penguin Books Ltd, 80 Strand, London, WC2R 0RL, UK
Penguin Books Australia Ltd, 707 Collins Street, Melbourne,
Victoria 3008, Australia
Penguin Books (NZ), 67 Apollo Drive, Rosedale, Auckland
0632, New Zealand (a divison of Pearson New Zealand Ltd)

ISBN 978-0-71819-785-8
001

Printed in China

This book is based on the
TV Series 'Peppa Pig'
'Peppa Pig' is created by
Neville Astley and Mark Baker
Peppa Pig © Astley Baker Davies/
Entertainment One UK Limited 2003.

www.peppapig.com

ALWAYS LEARNING   **PEARSON**

Once upon a time, it was nearly Peppa's birthday, and she was on the telephone to Suzy Sheep.

"I'm going to have a party! And Daddy is doing a magic show!" Peppa told Suzy excitedly.

"I hope you don't mind, Daddy," Mummy Pig whispered, "I promised Peppa."
"Ho! Ho! Not at all!" Daddy Pig replied. "Of course The Amazing
Mysterio will make a special appearance!"
George was excited too. He *loved* parties and magic shows.

Peppa wanted to start planning her party straight away.
She asked Mummy Pig if she could invite all of her friends.
"Yes!' Mummy Pig said. "And George can invite some too."
"But George's friends are little!" Peppa said.
Mummy Pig told Peppa that she could teach
George's friends all the party games.
"Oh, yes! I am very good at that!" agreed Peppa.

Soon it was Peppa's birthday.
It was very early in the morning but
Peppa was already wide awake.
"Wake up! It's my birthday!" Peppa
shouted, bouncing on Mummy and
Daddy Pig's bed.
"What time is it?" asked
Mummy Pig.

Daddy Pig checked.
It was five o'clock
in the morning!

At seven o'clock, everyone was dressed and ready for breakfast.
"OK, let's get your birthday started," Mummy Pig said.
George passed Peppa her birthday present.

"Happy birthday, Peppa!"

Mummy and Daddy Pig said together.
"Snort! Snort!" said George.
Peppa tore off the pretty paper excitedly. It was
a pink polka-dot dress for Teddy!
"Thank you, everyone!" she cried.

Snort!

Ding-dong!

Ding-dong!
Peppa's friends had arrived! **"Happy birthday, Peppa!"** shouted
Candy Cat, Suzy Sheep, Danny Dog, Rebecca Rabbit, Zoe Zebra, Emily
Elephant and Pedro Pony.

George's little friends were there too. "Squeak! Trumpet! Neigh! Neigh!" said Richard Rabbit, Edmond Elephant, and Zuzu and Zaza Zebra.

Peppa explained how to play Musical Statues to George
and his friends.
"You have to dance when the music is playing, and
when it stops, freeze like a statue."
Click. Danny Dog pressed 'play' on the stereo.
But no one moved.
"You've got to dance!" Peppa called.
The little children started to dance.
Heads, shoulders, knees and toes . . .

Click

Click. Danny Dog turned off the stereo. George, Richard, Edmond, Zuzu and Zaza froze.
"You're moving, George!" Peppa said. "You're out!"
"Waaaaaaaaaaaah!" George cried very loudly.
One by one, all of George's friends were out except for Zaza.
"Zaza is the winner!" Emily Elephant announced.

Click

"Here's your medal," she added, looping the red ribbon around the little zebra's neck.
"It's made of real plastic gold," Candy Cat said.
"Waaaaaaaaaah!" cried George, Richard, Edmond and Zuzu. They wanted medals too.

Daddy Pig hurried in to
cheer everyone up with
a magic show.
"Peppa," whispered
Daddy Pig, "remember
to introduce me as
The Amazing Mysterio!"

"Ladies and gentlemen . . . it's Magic Daddy!" said Peppa.
"Hooray!" The audience cheered and clapped.
Magic Daddy took off his top hat and waved a hand over it,
ready to perform his first trick . . .

"...Ta-da!"
Teddy appeared from Magic Daddy's hat!
The children clapped again.
"For my next trick, I need a helper from the audience,'
said Magic Daddy.
Everyone put their hand up.

Magic Daddy chose Suzy Sheep.
"OK, Suzy, here are three coloured balls,"
he said, turning his back and closing his eyes.
"You have to secretly choose one while I'm
not looking."
Suzy picked up the red ball.
"Abracadabra . . ." Magic Daddy said.

". . . You chose yellow!"
Magic Daddy guessed.
"No," said Suzy Sheep.
Magic Daddy guessed again.
"You chose . . . blue!"
"No," Suzy Sheep said.
Magic Daddy had one more guess.
"You chose . . . red!"
"Yes!" Suzy Sheep said.
"Hooray!" the children cheered
and clapped.

Yes!

Peppa wasn't sure Magic Daddy should have said all *three* colours, but she clapped anyway.
Next, Magic Daddy turned off the lights.
"Close your eyes, no peeping. Now, say the magic word!"
"Abracadabra!" the children cried.

Abracadabra!

Abracadabra!

"Open your eyes!" cried Magic Daddy, turning the lights back on.
The children opened their eyes. **"Ooh!"** they gasped.
Mummy Pig was holding a delicious-looking cake with four
candles on it!
"My banana birthday cake!" cried Peppa.
"Blow the candles out, Peppa," Mummy Pig said.

"And don't forget to make a wish," Daddy Pig added.
Peppa squeezed her eyes shut and wished very hard.
Then – whoosh! – she blew them all out at once!

"**Hooray!**" cheered her friends. "**Happy birthday, Peppa!**"
Suzy Sheep asked her what she'd wished, but Peppa wouldn't tell
– she really wanted her birthday wish to come true!
"And finally!" announced Magic Daddy. "I have one last trick to amaze
you with . . . **Abracadabra!**"
He pulled a present from his top hat and handed it to Peppa.

Peppa squealed, tearing off the paper and opening the box. Inside was a beautiful pair of yellow wellies!

"Right! Boots on, everyone!" Mummy Pig called.
All the children ran to the hall to put on their wellies.
"What's happening?" Peppa asked. "Why has everyone
brought their boots?"

Peppa, George and their friends followed Mummy
Pig out into the garden. Peppa was so excited she
couldn't stop skipping!

Daddy Pig and George quickly picked up two buckets and poured water all over the grass.

"Surprise!" everyone
shouted. "Happy birthday, Peppa!"
"Puddles! Hooray!" Peppa yelled,
leaping in, and jumping up and
down. "My birthday wish came
true! Come on, everyone!"

Mummy Pig, Daddy Pig, George, George's friends and Peppa's friends all jumped in. Everyone loves jumping in muddy puddles!
"This is the best birthday **ever!**" shouted Peppa. "Snort!"